Advent

KIMBERLY DERTING and SHELLI R. JOHANNES

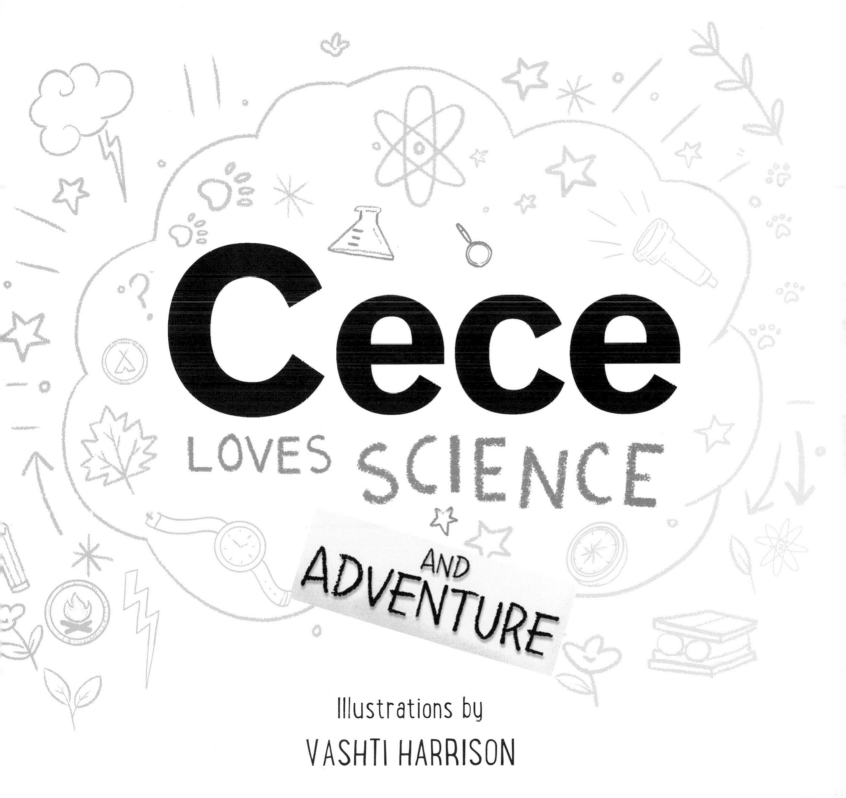

Cece
LOVES SCIENCE

AND ADVENTURE

Illustrations by
VASHTI HARRISON

Greenwillow Books, *An Imprint of* HarperCollins*Publishers*

Cece loved being an Adventure Girl
almost as much as she loved science.
She couldn't wait to earn her camping pin.
There was so much science she could explore
in nature.

In the past, Cece had run into trouble earning her Adventure Girl pins.

The sewing challenge had her in stitches.

The jewelry activity tangled her in knots.

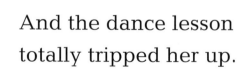

And the dance lesson totally tripped her up.

But this time, Cece could finally put science to work!

Cece packed everything
on the checklist.

Then she remembered what her science teacher,
Ms. Curie, said: "Real scientists are always
prepared."
So Cece packed a few extra things, just in case.

Cece's friends Daisy and Caroline were Adventure
Girls, too.
Cece's mother was the group leader.
And Cece's dog, Einstein, was their unofficial mascot.

When Cece's mother saw Cece's heavy bag,
she smiled. "Looks like you had an extra checklist."
"It's good to be prepared," said Cece. "Wait! We need
one s'more thing."
"Sweet!" cheered Caroline and Daisy.

Adventure Girls
Camping Pin Worksheet

- ☑ Plan your adventure and pack

- ☐ Set up your campsite

- ☐ Go on a nature hike with friends

- ☐ Make a list of different plants and animals you find

- ☐ Make a map of your wilderness route

- ☐ Have fun!

- ☐ make tons of s'mores

When the Adventure Girls reached the campground,
Cece's mother handed them the camping pin worksheets.
Cece read the next task out loud. "Set up your campsite."

"Putting up this tent will be a breeze," Cece whispered to Einstein.

But the wind did not agree!

The Adventure Girls worked together as a team.

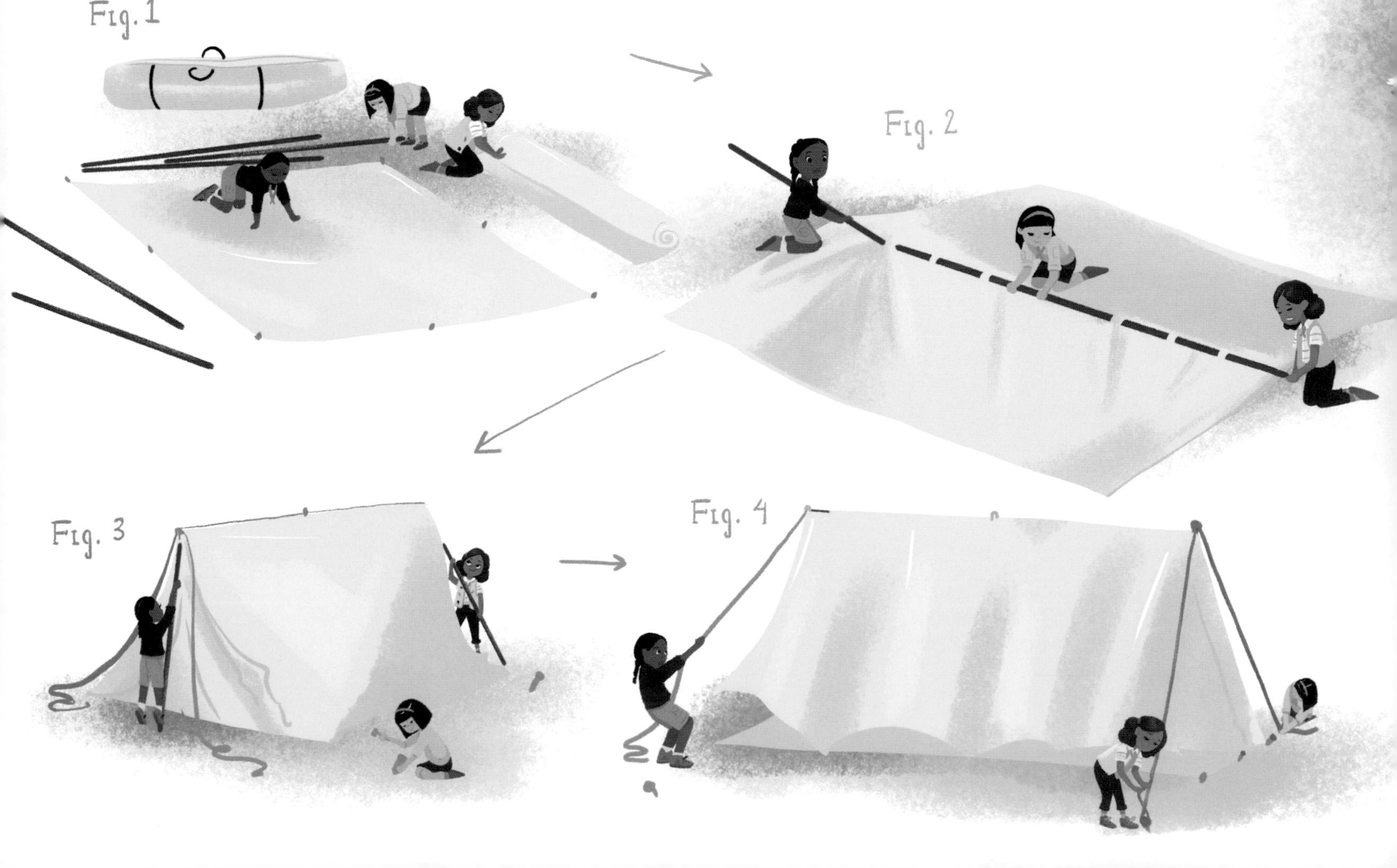

Fig. 1

Fig. 2

Fig. 3

Fig. 4

Finally, they had built
a home away from home.

"I think you've earned a snack," said Cece's mom.
"Einstein gets one, too!"

Caroline looked at her worksheet. "Time to go on a nature hike," she said.

Daisy smiled. "This is the fun part."

"I'll take pictures to track our route," said Cece, grabbing her digital camera.

The Adventure Girls headed into the wilderness.
Daisy found the perfect hiking stick.
Caroline picked flowers.
And Einstein led the pack.

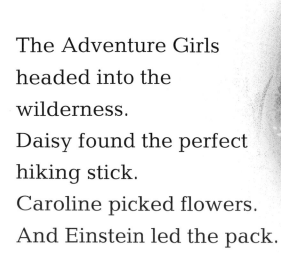

Cece took pictures of landmarks along the trail—

a twisty oak tree,

a dry riverbed,

and a fork in the path.

She also took one of a huge boulder that looked like a gnome with a mossy beard.

All of a sudden, the sky grew darker.

"Uh-oh," said Daisy.

"I hope it doesn't rain," said Caroline.

"It's okay, Adventure Girls," said Cece's mom.
"Don't worry."

But Cece wasn't so sure.
She studied the gray clouds and remembered
what she'd learned about weather during
Ms. Curie's meteorology lesson.
"Mom, I think a storm is coming," Cece said.

The wind picked up and thunder boomed in the distance.

"Cece, you might be right," said her mom.

"Maybe the storm is far away," said Daisy.

"How can we tell?" asked Caroline.

Cece knew science could solve almost any problem. She told her friends about a trick Ms. Curie had taught her. "If we see lightning, we count the seconds until we hear thunder. Every five seconds equals one mile."

Just then, lightning flashed across the sky.

Daisy looked at her watch and they started counting.

"One Mississippi, two Mississippi, three Mississippi . . ."

When they reached twenty, thunder rumbled again.

"That means the storm is still four miles away," Cece said.

"When thunder roars, go indoors!" said Cece's mom.

"We'd better head back to camp."

Cece's mom tried to map the route on her phone. "My GPS isn't working," she said. "Maybe it's the storm!" said Daisy.

"I know," said Cece, holding up her camera. "We can be detectives and use my pictures to make a map."

Cece got a notebook and pencils from her backpack.
The Adventure Girls drew a map and marked the
spot where they thought their campsite would be.

Suddenly, it started to pour.

"Oh no!" yelled Daisy. "We're getting soaked!"

"We need to find someplace dry," said Cece's mom.

"I know! We can build a shelter," said Cece.

"Our rain ponchos can be the roof," said Caroline.

"Daisy, let's use your walking stick as a tentpole," said Cece. Soon, the Adventure Girls had built a shelter.

They climbed inside and huddled together to stay dry.

Once the storm had passed, Cece's mom said, "Time to go!"

"How long will it take?" Daisy asked. "I'm hungry."

"How far is it?" Caroline asked. "I'm tired."

"We can easily figure it out," said Cece. She showed them the photo of the twisty oak tree.

"That was really close to camp!" said Daisy.

"The time stamp says 1:00," said Caroline.

Cece pulled up their group picture. "Look! This one was taken at 1:45." Caroline pointed to the gnome rock. "And we took it right there."

"So if we subtract 1:00 from 1:45, that means we're about forty-five minutes away from camp," said Cece.
"That's not far at all!" said Daisy.
"S'mores, here we come!" said Caroline.

Forty-five minutes later, the Adventure Girls arrived
at their camp, ready to eat.
But when Cece looked inside the tent, she found
an empty marshmallow bag.
"Einstein!" Cece's mom scolded.

"Mom, I don't think it was Einstein," said Cece,
 pointing to tracks in the mud. "Look!"
"Something stole our snack," said Caroline.
"That means there's no s'more for us," said Daisy.

Cece held up the graham crackers and chocolate bars. "We'll just have to make chocolate sandwiches," she said.

"The Adventure Girls did a great job today," said Cece's mom. "You all definitely earned your camping pins. And because you solved problems using science, technology, engineering, and math, I'm awarding you STEM pins, too. Even Einstein."

"Hooray!" cheered Cece. "Science rules!"

Daisy and Caroline hugged Cece.

"You saved the day," said Daisy.

"Thanks, Cece," said Caroline.

Cece's mom smiled. "Since you worked so well together, I'm also giving you a special pin," she said. "For teamwork."

Cece smiled. "Solving problems is always easier when you have a super team!"

daisy caroline CECE

STEM PIN WORKSHEET

- STEM = Science, Technology, Engineering, and Math

  STEM also stands for
  Super Team, Einstein,
  and Mom!!!

- Science—the study of the natural world.

  Counted lightning Strikes to
  figure out how far away
  the Storm was

- Technology—the use of science in solving problems, usually involving something that was created by humans.

  made a map from pictures
  on the camera so we could find
  our way back to camp

- Engineering—the branch of science and technology concerned with designing and building structures.

  Built a shelter to Keep us dry!

- Math—the study of numbers, quantities, and measurements.

  - Used the time stamps on the
  - pictures to calculate how far
    we were from camp

Adventure Girls

Cece's Science Facts

- **Cloud**—A collection of tiny water particles or ice crystals that float in the air. The three basic types of clouds are stratus, cirrus, and cumulus.

- **Einstein**—My dog and unofficial mascot. He was named after Albert Einstein, a famous scientist who had crazy hair and tons of theories in math and physics.

- **GPS**—Stands for "Global Positioning System," or a really cool way we use satellites to map the world.

- **Lightning**—Super-amazing electrical charges that light up the sky during a storm. Each bolt can contain up to 1 billion volts of electricity. That's a lot of energy!

- **Meteorology**—The study of the atmosphere and weather. A meteorologist tells us if we're going to have sunny skies or need to pack an umbrella.

- **Ms. Curie**—My teacher, who amazingly has the same last name as the famous scientist Marie Curie, the first woman to win the Nobel Prize and the only woman to win it twice—in physics AND in chemistry!

- **Rain**—Water that falls in drops from the clouds and makes awesome puddles to jump in (with rain boots, of course!).

- **Shelter**—A place or structure that gives protection against weather or danger.

- **STEM**—Stands for science, technology, engineering, and mathematics. Sometimes it includes art and is called STEAM. (I think STEM also stands for **S**uper **T**eam, **E**instein, and **M**om.)

- **Storm**—Bad weather that could include rain, snow, hail, really bad winds, or sometimes all of the above. Einstein hates storms!

- **Time stamp**—A record, often digital, of the time or date an event occurs.

- **Thunder**—The sound caused by lightning, usually a really loud boom.

- **Wind**—This is air in motion that blows stuff around, including tents.

- **Weather**—Conditions in the atmosphere that may include wind, storms, rain, and changes in temperature.

To all the adventurous women who dare
to explore the unknown—K. D. & S. R. J.

For Carrie—V. H.

Cece Loves Science and Adventure
Text copyright © 2019 by Kimberly Derting and Shelli R. Johannes
Illustrations copyright © 2019 by Vashti Harrison
All rights reserved. Manufactured in China. For information
address HarperCollins Children's Books, a division of
HarperCollins Publishers, 195 Broadway, New York, NY 10007.
www.harpercollinschildrens.com

The full-color art was created in Adobe Photoshop™.
The text type is Candida.

Library of Congress Cataloging-in-Publication Data
Names: Derting, Kimberly, author. | Johannes, S. R., author. | Harrison,
  Vashti, illustrator.
Title: Cece loves science and adventure / by Kimberly Derting and Shelli R.
  Johannes ; illustrated by Vashti Harrison.
Description: First edition. | New York, NY : Greenwillow Books, an imprint of
  HarperCollinsPublishers, [2019] | Summary: When Cece and her Adventure
  Girls troop face a sudden thunderstorm, they use science, technology, engineering,
  and math to solve problems and make their way safely back to camp.
Identifiers: LCCN 2018030510 | ISBN 9780062499622 (hardcover)
Subjects: | CYAC: Scouting (Youth activity)—Fiction. | Camping—Fiction. |
  Thunderstorms—Fiction. | Scientists—Fiction.
Classification: LCC PZ7.D4468 Cec 2019 | DDC [E]—dc23 LC record available
  at https://lccn.loc.gov/2018030510

19 20 21 22 23 SCP 10 9 8 7 6 5 4 3 2 1
First Edition
Greenwillow Books